MUD FLAT APRIL FOOL

JAMES STEVENSON

Greenwillow Books   New York

Watercolor paints and a black pen
were used for the full-color art.
The text type is Veljovic Medium.
Copyright © 1998 by James Stevenson
All rights reserved. No part of this book
may be reproduced or utilized in any form
or by any means, electronic or mechanical,
including photocopying, recording, or by
any information storage and retrieval system,
without permission in writing from the
Publisher, Greenwillow Books, a division of
William Morrow & Company, Inc.,
1350 Avenue of the Americas, New York, NY 10019.
http://www.williammorrow.com
Printed in Singapore by Tien Wah Press
First Edition 10 9 8 7 6 5 4 3 2 1

Library of Congress Cataloging-in-Publication Data
Stevenson, James, (date)
Mud Flat April Fool / by James Stevenson.
p.   cm.
Summary: The animal inhabitants of Mud Flat
play April Fools' Day tricks on each other
involving flying saucers, disappearing neighbors,
and water-squirting flowers.
ISBN 0-688-15163-9 (trade)
ISBN 0-688-15164-7 (lib. bdg.)
[1. April Fools' Day—Fiction.   2. Animals—Fiction.]
I. Title.   PZ7.S84748Mrf   1998   [E]—dc21   97-10014   CIP   AC

CONTENTS

1
The Message

"Mr. Goodhue!" said Alice.

"Yes, Alice?" said Mr. Goodhue.

"I have a message for you," said Alice.

"Who is it from?" said Mr. Goodhue.

"One of the little green creatures," said Alice.

"What little green creatures?" said Mr. Goodhue.

"The ones that climbed out of the flying saucer," said Alice.

"What flying saucer was that?" said Mr. Goodhue.

"The big one that landed in the field last night," said Alice.

"My goodness," said Mr. Goodhue.
"I missed that. I guess I was asleep."
"Here's the message," said Alice.

Mr. Goodhue read the message aloud:

"You sure got me that time, Alice,"
said Mr. Goodhue.

"May I have that note back, please?"
said Alice. "If it works this well, I may
want to try it again."
"I can understand that," said Mr. Goodhue.

2

Mr. Duffy

Mr. Duffy was taking off his bedroom
slippers and putting on his shoes.
"Good morning, Mr. Duffy," said Matt.
"Are you going somewhere?"

"As a matter of fact, I am, Matt," said
Mr. Duffy. "This is the day each year
that I catch the local train to Rocky
Ledge and pay a call on my great-aunt
Flobelia."

"I guess you'll miss April Fools' Day,"
said Zack.

"Can't be helped," said Mr. Duffy.

"See you later, boys."

He walked off up the path.

A few minutes later Mrs. Crane came
along, carrying her grocery bag.
"Mrs. Crane! Mrs. Crane!" called Matt.
"A scary thing just happened!"
"Really?" said Mrs. Crane. "What?"
"Mr. Duffy disappeared in a puff
of green smoke!" said Matt.
"Look," said Zack. "All that's left of
him are his slippers."
"That's terrible," said Mrs. Crane.
"Especially *today*."

"Why today?" said Matt.

"Because today is the day each year that
Mr. Duffy catches the local
train to Rocky Ledge to pay
a call on his great-aunt
Flobelia," said Mrs. Crane.
She walked away.

"We're going to have to try harder," said Matt.
"I think you're right," said Zack.

3
The Daffodil

"Look what I found in the attic," said George.
"An old squirting rose."
"How does it work?" said Tim.
"You'll see," said George. "Here comes Lila—
 just watch."

"Hi, George," said Lila. "Nice rose
 you've got there."
"Thank you, Lila," said George.
"Would you like to smell it?"
"Oh, yes," said Lila. "That would be nice."

"Put your nose good and close," said George,
"so you can really smell it."

"I don't smell anything yet," said Lila.
George squirted the rose.

"April Fool!" said George.
"What a great trick," said Tim.

"What happened to you, Lila?" said Benny.

"I got tricked by George and his
 squirting rose," said Lila.

"Why don't you play a trick on George?"
 said Benny.

"I don't know any tricks," said Lila.

"We'll think of one while you dry off,"
 said Benny.

 Lila and Benny sat down to think.

Later that morning George was walking
around, looking for people to squirt, when
he saw Lila standing by the tree.
"Hello, George," said Lila. She was holding
a daffodil.
"Hello, Lila," said George. "No hard feelings
about my squirting rose trick, I hope?"
"Oh, no," said Lila. "In fact, I have just
picked a lovely daffodil for you."

"That's nice of you," said George.
"Just a friendly gesture," said Lila.

"I would suspect a trick, of course,"
said George. "But this is just a plain,
ordinary daffodil."

"Exactly," said Lila.

"Thank you," said George.

"See you later," said Lila.

She walked away.

George was admiring his daffodil when . . .

Benny leaned out of the tree and dumped
a bucket of water on him.

George stood in the puddle, staring at
the daffodil.

"This daffodil really works," said George.
"But I sure can't figure out how."

4
The Trip
Around the World

"I know you snails don't care much about speed," said Megan. "But I have to tell you— I am the fastest bird in the world."

"You are?" said Kate.

"Really?" said Martha.

"Yes," said Megan. "I am now going to fly around the world, and I will be back in five minutes."

"That's fast," said Kate.

"Very fast," said Martha.

Megan took off.

"She thinks going fast is all that matters," said Kate.

"Want to fool Megan?" said Martha.

"Why not?" said Kate.

A few minutes later Megan fell to the ground
behind them.

"Whew!" she said. "That was some trip!"

"You went all the way around the world?"
said Martha.

"Absolutely!" said Megan. "In less than five
minutes. You saw me take off."

"Yes," said Kate. "But that was six weeks ago."

"More like two months," said Martha.

"We haven't seen you in ever so long,"
  said Kate.

"Maybe you've been flying too much.
  You should get a little rest."

"Maybe you're right," said Megan.

"April Fool!" said Kate.
"April Fool!" said Martha.
"You fooled me," said Megan.
"Slowly but surely," said Kate.

5
Mrs. Beekley's Party

"Look out, Zack," said Matt.

"There's old Mrs. Beekley. She's always
 very cross."

"Are you boys playing tricks on people?"
 said Mrs. Beekley.

"No, ma'am," said Zack. "Hardly at all."

"You think it's fun to fool people, do you?"
 she said.

"Oh, no," said Matt. "We don't enjoy it."

"We just do it," said Zack.

"Well, I'm giving a big party tonight,"
 said Mrs. Beekley. "Very big—ice cream,
 balloons, music—everything. You're both
 invited."

"Oh, thank you, Mrs. Beekley," said Zack.

"We'll be there, Mrs. Beekley," said Matt.

"Promptly at six," she said, and walked
 away.

"Does she think we'll fall for that?"
 said Matt.
 He and Zack
 started laughing.

"Ice cream!"
 said Matt.

"Balloons!"
 said Zack.

6

The Singing Tree

"I have a good idea for how to fool Doris,"
 said Danny.

"How?" said Joey.

"You climb up that tree and hide in that
 hole," said Danny.

"I can do that," said Joey. "Then what?"

"When Doris comes along," said Danny,
"I will tell her that this is a Singing Tree."

"And what do I do?" said Joey.

"You sing," said Danny. "You know, wind-
in-the-leaves music."

"You mean, like *woo-woo-woo*?" said Joey.

"Fine," said Danny. "Here comes Doris—
get in the hole!"

Joey ran up the tree and hid in the hole.

"Hi, Doris," said Danny.

"Hello, Danny," said Doris. "What are
 you doing?"
"I am listening to the strange and
 mysterious music of the Singing
 Tree," said Danny.
"I don't hear anything," said Doris.
"Put your ear close to the tree,"
 said Danny. "You will be amazed."
"Nothing so far," said Doris.
"The mysterious music doesn't happen
 all the time," said Danny.
"I guess not,"
 said Doris.
"But it should happen
 soon!" said Danny
 in a loud voice.
"'Take me out to the
 ball game,'" sang
 Joey. "'Take me out
 with the crowd . . .'"

"That is not a tree singing," said Doris.
"That is more like a squirrel singing."
"April Fool!" said Joey.
"What happened to *woo-woo-woo?*"
 said Danny.
"I thought a real song coming out of a tree
 would be even more amazing," said Joey.
"You never know," said Danny.
"A real tree would probably
 go *woo-woo-woo,*" said Doris.

7

Morning at Mud Flat

Matt and Zack went down
the main path of Mud Flat
to see their friend Brian.

When they got near Brian's house,
they saw him sitting on the porch
with a blanket pulled over him.

"There's something weird about
  Brian," whispered Matt.
"He doesn't look right."
"Brian!" called Zack.
"Is something wrong?"
"Yes," said Brian. "When I got up
  this morning, my head was on
  backward."

"I thought you looked different," said Matt.
"Does it hurt?"
"You have to come around back if you
  want to talk to me," said Brian.

Matt went around to the back
of Brian's chair, while Zack
stared at Brian's feet.

"How could your head get turned
around backward?" said Matt.

"I don't know," said Brian.
"But maybe I can twist it around to
the front again."
"Are you sure that's a good idea?"
said Matt.
"Well, I certainly don't want to walk
around with my head on backward
for the rest of my life," said Brian.

"Be careful," said Zack.
"Here goes!" said Brian.

There was a loud screeching noise.
Zack and Matt shut their eyes.
"Hey," said Brian. "I'm all well!"
Zack and Matt opened their eyes.

Brian was standing there, looking
the way he always did.
"That must be a very rare thing,"
said Matt. "A backward head."
"You're right," said Brian. "It only
happens on April Fools' Day."

8
Newt's Dollar

"I'm doing my old dollar-on-a-string trick,"
 said Newt. "It always works."
"How do you do it?" said Ashley.
"I put the dollar on the path," said Newt.
"When somebody tries to pick it up,
 I yank the string."

"Here comes Mr. Hawley," said Dorothy.
"Watch what happens," said Newt.

Mr. Hawley tried to pick up the dollar.
Newt pulled the string.
The dollar flew through the air.
"What in the world . . . ?" said Mr. Hawley.
"April Fool, Mr. Hawley!" said Newt.

"That worked perfectly," said Ashley.

"Of course," said Newt. "It always does."

Suddenly the dollar flew out of Newt's hand.

"Where's my dollar?" cried Newt.
"I believe it's flying over Mr. Wilson's barn,"
 said Ashley.

"April Fool!" called Dorothy.

9

Dorothy

"I think I'll try Newt's trick," said Dorothy,
"now that I have Newt's dollar."

She put the dollar
on the path and hid
behind the tree,
holding the string.

A long time went by.
Nobody came.

"This is very boring,"
said Dorothy. "I don't think
I can stand it any more."

"Oh, good!" said Dorothy.
"Here comes Mr. Mullins."

"Looks like somebody lost a dollar,"
said Mr. Mullins. "I'll tell everybody
I meet, in case it's their dollar."
Then he walked on.

"I hate this trick," said Dorothy.
"I can't wait to give Newt his
dollar back."

10
Party

That night Zack and Matt were sitting
on the steps of Zack's porch.
Mr. Goodhue walked by.
Mrs. Crane walked by.
Then Alice and Joey and Doris
and Newt and Danny.

"Where's everybody going?" said Zack.

"To Mrs. Beekley's party," said Alice.

"Didn't you get invited?" said Doris.

"Of course we got invited," said Matt.

"We were practically the first ones,"
 said Zack.

"Then come on," said Newt.

Matt and Zack joined the parade.

"I hear music," said Matt.

"I smell food," said Zack.

"I see balloons," said Matt.

The house was full of people.
Mrs. Beekley greeted Matt and Zack
at the door. "Hello, boys," she said.
"Mrs. Beekley," said Matt,
"Zack and I didn't think
you were really having a party.
We thought you were trying to fool us."

"Well, I *did* fool you, didn't I?"
said Mrs. Beekley. "April Fool!"
"It was a good trick," said Zack.
"Come on in," said Mrs. Beekley.
"The party's just begun!"